The Wedding of Jessica Packwood and Lucius Vladescu

Beth Fantaskey

DEDICATION

To all of the wonderful readers of *Jessica's Guide to Dating on the Dark Side* and *Jessica Rules the Dark Side* who requested the wedding in print for their bookshelves.

ACKNOWLEDGMENTS

Several years ago, I developed an interactive event that allowed readers to help me plan a "wedding" for Princess Antanasia Dragomir – aka Jessica Packwood – and Prince Lucius Vladescu. The result was a fun, hectic few weeks that created a community of reader-bridesmaids and resulted in this story. I want to thank everyone who took part in the original event, as well as all of those readers who've requested actual copies of the novella. Last but not least, I want to thank web designer Lieucretia Swain, who stayed up until many a midnight to make sure the original chapters were posted on my website by the promised deadlines. You are all the best.

CHAPTER 1

My best friend – if I could still call her that, like I hoped – Mindy Stankowicz looked completely baffled as crowds of Romanians who knew where they were going pushed past her to get to the baggage carousels at Bucharest's busy *Aeroportul Internaţional Henri Coandă*.

I knew that I should rush over and help Min, but I held back, just watching as she searched the crowd for me, her eyes now and then darting to signs covered with a language that my brief time in Romania hadn't prepared me to understand, either.

Bagaje pierdute. Conexiune gara. Carucioare bagaje.

Mindy took a hesitant step forward – then stopped again, obviously not sure where to go, and I still didn't move, either. My feet seemed bolted down as I tried to sort out all of the emotions that rushed through me just to see a friend from my recent past, someone who'd witnessed everything that had happened in high school, from the day Lucius Vladescu had walked into my life to the night I'd feared he'd been taken away from me, forever.

Looking back on our last months of school, I still wasn't sure if Mindy had deserted me, or if I'd abandoned her as things with Lucius had gotten more intense. Mindy had wanted to help me deal with all that I'd been going through with Lucius and Faith Crosse and Jake Zinn, but I'd pushed her away, scared to confide the truth about my feelings for Lucius – and the truth about what he was. Not to mention what *I* was becoming. Still, the day that Mindy had yanked her arm away from me in gym class – sort of renouncing our friendship – I'd been hurt.

Who had been the worse friend?

Standing in the middle of the crowded airport, surrounded by Romanian travelers who were all hauling their luggage off spinning baggage carousels as announcements were made in numerous languages, Mindy suddenly looked *scared*, and I remembered one crucial detail from our shared history.

On the night that Lucius had almost been destroyed – on my 18th birthday, when nearly everybody else, even my parents, in a way, had turned their backs on me and him – Mindy had called to warn me that he was in deep trouble.

She'd had her doubts about Lucius, feared that he might even be hurting me, but in the end she'd come through and tried to save his life, because she'd already known that I loved him.

Maybe, if I hadn't shown up in the barn that night and tried to intervene, things would have gone a little differently. Maybe Ethan Strausser would have grabbed the stake instead of Jake, and Lucius would be gone...

All at once my feet were freed, and I wasn't just walking toward Mindy, I was running. And without even thinking about how things might be awkward between us – I was a vampire, for crying out loud, and we hadn't seen each other since my transformation – I shoved through the crowds and held open my arms, just as Mindy saw me, too, and threw her own arms wide, so we both crashed into each other and started crying so hard that we didn't even have the time or the composure to say "hello."

We hung onto each other for a long time, ignoring the people who pushed past us, some cursing mildly in Romanian. And when we finally calmed down, I blurted out the question I'd been wanting to pose, but had been too scared to voice, thinking maybe it was enough just to ask Mindy to fly to Romania for the wedding of a friend she might not even like anymore.

"Will you be my maid of honor? Please?"

Mindy pulled away from me and dragged her fingers under her eyes, which were dripping mascara all over her cheeks, then said, with a shaky, still half-teary smile, "Jeez, Jess, I thought you'd never ask!"

I wiped at my own face, trying to clear away some of my tears, too. "I was afraid –"

That you'd say no. That you couldn't in good conscience support my marriage to a vampire. That we weren't friends like that anymore.

But before I could find the right words, Mindy squeezed my arm, stopping me from saying more. "Who else is gonna do your hair on the most important day of your life, Jess?" she teased. "Huh?"

For some reason I almost started to cry again – but I was laughing, too. "Nobody but you," I promised, knowing that everything that had happened between us, all of the weirdness, had been fixed.

Or maybe there was one more thing to say, because suddenly Mindy got serious. "You're really a –" She glanced around, probably checking to see if there were any English speakers who might overhear. Then she leaned close and whispered, "Vampire?"

I straightened a little, not wanting to hide what I was or act like I was ashamed. "Yes. I am."

Mindy studied my face for a long time, like she needed to see that I was still really, truly me, and not just some bloodsucking creature who would be beyond her understanding. Gradually, I saw her smile not only return, but get steadier and warmer, like she was setting aside her last reservations about me. About us. "That's cool," she finally said with a nod. "That's okay."

I hadn't known that I needed anybody's endorsement, but I guessed I needed Mindy's, because it felt good to hear somebody say that out loud.

What I was now... It really was okay.

"Thanks," I said, as my own smile got even bigger.

I'd been ecstatic about marrying Lucius, but having my best friend back... It filled some empty place in my heart, and although we were pretty much adults, and I was about to be married, I reached out and held her hand, just like we used to do when we were little kids on the playground.

"Let's get your bags," I suggested, pulling her toward the correct carousel, where most of the luggage had already been claimed. As we stepped up, though, I saw three big, new-looking, faux Louis Vuitton suitcases conspicuously taking the ride around for probably the twentieth time. When they reached us, Mindy let go of my hand and hauled one, then another, off the belt, and I hurried to grab the remaining bag before it could spin by again.

As the heavy suitcase thudded to my feet, I looked at Mindy, confused. "*Three* pieces of luggage? But I thought you can only stay for three days, tops?"

Mindy looked at me like I was the one who was out of my mind. "This is the biggest event of your life," she reminded me. "It's gonna take a lot of hair product!"

I started grinning like crazy then, feeling completely happy. I was about to marry Lucius, and Mindy really was back.

"Come on," I said, starting to wheel the suitcase I'd claimed toward the exit. "Lucius has a driver waiting for us, and we have lots to do."

"I'm right behind you," Mindy promised, hurrying along with her two bags wobbling in tow. "Can't wait!"

I looked over at her and we shared a smile that summed up about fifteen years of friendship and all the hopes and dreams we'd had as girls about falling in love and getting married and living happily ever after.

Then I faced forward and led us both toward the waiting car.

The wedding was officially underway.

CHAPTER 2

"I'm thinking a classic updo," Mindy said, her head bent as she leafed through the pages of a special bridal edition of *Celebrity Hairstyle* magazine. "Depending, of course, on your headpiece."

I was torn between checking out the options and watching the passing scenery from the back seat of the Lexus SUV that Lucius had provided for our ride from the airport. Apparently he'd anticipated how much Mindy would pack, because the SUV had more storage than the other vehicles in the Vladescu's well-stocked garage... the contents of which would soon be at my beck and call, too, hard as that still was to believe.

Outside the window, the dramatic vistas of the rising Carpathians unfolded, and now and then when we rounded a curve on the steep mountain road, I'd find myself staring at nothing but sky and grab the seat, because I still wasn't used to those hairpin turns, either.

Do I really LIVE here?

"Jess?" Mindy tapped my sleeve. "I asked about your headpiece. It's gonna be a tiara, right? I mean, it has to be a tiara!"

I turned to see Min's eyes gleaming at the prospect of being part of an honest-to-goodness royal wedding – the kind we'd never really thought would happen for either one of us, in spite of what all our favorite Disney movies had taught us to expect. "Yes, it's a tiara," I confirmed, thinking Mindy might actually be more excited than me about the wedding, itself. I couldn't wait to be married to Lucius, but I was nervous, too, about the ceremony.

Would I follow all the proper protocol?

Would the guests have a good time?

And most importantly, would any of my relatives – Dragomir or Vladescu – cause any trouble? Because that was definitely possible.

"I can't wait to see the dress!" Mindy said, returning her attention to the magazine on her lap. "I bet it's beautiful!"

"You'll see it tomorrow," I promised, hoping she'd like it. And I hoped Lucius would like the gown I'd chosen. I'd designed it myself with the help of his Romanian tailor, and it was a little unconventional. But I'd wanted to wear something that would remind him of a certain moment we'd shared, before I'd even admitted to liking him.

I could still hear his voice as he'd stood behind me in a Pennsylvania dress shop, his fingers twisted up into my curly hair. *"Don't ever again say that you are not 'valuable,' Antanasia. Or not beautiful..."*

That was the first time I'd felt remotely like the princess I was still trying to learn to be.

Getting nervous again, I resumed staring out the window and saw the rooftops of Sighisoara in the distance. It crossed my mind to suggest a slight detour, so I could show Mindy the charming, medieval town, just like my Uncle Dorin had done for me the first time I'd traveled to Romania. But at the last moment I kept my mouth shut, because there was something else that I was eager to show Mindy first, even more than the narrow, quaint streets that Lucius had roamed as a child.

Leaning forward, I tapped the driver's shoulder, then read from a note I'd had Lucius write for me, butchering the words with my poor accent. *"Se opreste cind ai lui Vladescu casa, te rog."*

Although Mindy glanced up from her magazine to give me an impressed look, I knew my pronunciation was way off. But the driver – one of the stern young guards who'd once pinned my arms in a dark forest – must have understood, because he nodded without taking his eyes off the twisting road and agreed, *"Da, bineinteles."*

"What's that all about?" Mindy asked, seeming remarkably comfortable for a girl taking her first ride in rural Romania with a vampiric chauffeur at the wheel of a luxury SUV. "What's up?"

"We're going to pull over in a second," I said. "There's something I want you to see."

"What...?"

Before Mindy could even finish her question, though, the SUV slowed and eased to the side of the road, and I pointed past my friend's shoulder, signaling for her to look out her own window.

She shifted in her seat and, when confronted with the view, had the reaction I'd expected, because I'd had it myself the first time Dorin had pulled over at almost that exact spot on the road. I still had the same reaction every time I saw the place that was going to be my home. The mixture of awe and disbelief and maybe a touch of fear that made your jaw actually drop and which left me, and now Mindy, unable to think, or say, anything more than...

"Is that place for real?"

CHAPTER 3

"You're really going to live *there*?" Mindy asked, without taking her eyes off the sprawling, soaring, Gothic Vladescu estate. She took a step closer to the edge of the precipice, and I grabbed her sleeve, not wanting her to tumble down into the steep, narrow valley that separated us from Lucius's home. But Mindy seemed too transfixed to even notice that I'd stopped her. "You're actually *getting married* there?"

It was hard to tell if I heard awe – or concern – in her voice. Maybe there was a mixture of both. Or maybe I was projecting my own conflicted emotions about my soon-to-be house onto my friend.

Letting go of Mindy's sleeve, I shaded my eyes against the setting sun and joined her in studying the massive castle.

The vast stone edifice, the size of a small – or maybe not-so-small – city block, was magnificent, without a doubt. Like something straight out of a fairy tale. And yet, as my eyes traced along the rambling exterior, which was punctuated by sharp, spike-like turrets and dominated by a tall watch tower, I couldn't help thinking, with more than a little misgiving, that fairy tales always had dark twists. Little kids got lost in desolate forests and stumbled across witches intent upon stuffing them into ovens. A handful of beans could lead to an encounter with an angry giant. And, as Lucius had reminded me in the shadow of the very stone walls I was observing, innocent girls could find themselves eaten by wolves, if they weren't always on guard...

Mindy interrupted my thoughts with a soft, low whistle. "That place is..."

She couldn't seem to articulate her thoughts, but I could finish them well enough.

Awesome.

Imposing.

Fearsome?

"Yes, I know," I agreed, dropping my hand and looking at Mindy. "It's almost too much for words."

She finally managed to tear her gaze away, too. "When you said you were getting married at Lucius's 'estate,' I didn't think you meant, like, an honest-to-goodness Cinderella, king-and-queen castle." Then she turned back to peer across the valley. "Where, exactly, will you get married in there? Is there, like, a special room just for weddings? Because it looks big enough to have a special room for everything."

I looked again at the castle, too, searching the towers and courtyards and tall, narrow windows – and trying to imagine the spot, myself.

"Lucius won't tell me," I admitted.

Mindy spun toward me, clearly shocked. "What? You're joking, right?"

Although she'd hadn't had a boyfriend yet – not unlike me not too long ago – she'd been planning her own wedding since we were about five years old. There was no way Melinda Stankowicz would ever let anybody – not even the love of her life – surprise her with a location for the most important night of her life. Especially not if she was getting married in a place that held collections of weapons and was splashed with bloodstains, for crying out loud.

No, Mindy would have insisted on seeing the room... or the chamber... or wherever, exactly, her groom intended to tie the knot.

"The only thing I know is that I haven't even seen the spot yet," I told her. "Lucius purposely kept it hidden from me when he showed me the rest of the castle." Including a labyrinth of buried chambers that could only be called a dungeon and a courtroom where one day I'd be expected to hand down judgments that might involve destruction.

"Jess, are you sure you don't want to see where you're actually exchanging vows?" Mindy asked, still aghast. I heard genuine concern – almost alarm – in her voice. "This is your wedding!"

"I know," I agreed. "Believe me – I've thought of that!"

I'd been very worried when Lucius had first suggested that I let him pick the location.

But when I'd brought up the topic of choosing where we'd marry, my future husband had said to me, "I know the perfect place." Then he'd arched his dark eyebrows, mischief in his black eyes, and asked, "Do you trust me, Antanasia?"

I'd looked into those complicated eyes for a long time, knowing that this was a once-in-an-eternity chance to choose where I'd get married... and thinking, just for a split second, that the vampire who stood before me had not too long ago surprised me with a stake pressed close to my heart.

Lucius had been smiling, teasing, but there'd been something serious in his expression, too, and I'd had a feeling that he was testing our bond, just a little. Then I'd begun to smile, too, mirroring Lucius's own grin…

"Jess – seriously!" Mindy's voice brought me back to the present again. "You're letting a guy – even a guy as cool as Lucius – make that decision?"

In spite of the twinges of apprehension I always felt in the shadow of the Vladescu estate, I found myself smiling again as I turned to Mindy and said, very honestly, "I trust him."

Then I glanced at my watch and realized that we needed to get moving. "Come on," I said, heading toward the waiting vehicle. "We need to get to the Dragomir estate – which is much less impressive," I warned her, so she wouldn't expect too much. "I'm sure you can't wait to clean up, and we both need to get dressed for dinner, then round up Mom and Dad, too. The last time I saw them, they were off on some hike in the mountains, looking for a medicinal plant Dad remembered harvesting the last time they were here."

"Your parents came?" Mindy asked. "Really?"

"Of course," I said, surprised that she would be surprised. This was my wedding. Then I remembered how Mom and Dad had tried to stop me from going to Lucius's aid on that terrible night when he'd almost been destroyed in the Zinn's barn. Mindy probably knew most of what had happened that evening, including how my parents had taken my car keys away, afraid that Lucius really had succumbed to his darker nature and bitten Faith Crosse.

"I forgave Mom and Dad a long time ago," I told Mindy, not even bothering to ask how much she knew for certain. "They were only trying to protect me. They didn't know how bad things were about to get for Lucius."

"Yeah, I guess not," Mindy agreed, as we reached the Lexus. But she held back a step, like she had something on her mind. "Jake…," she finally began, seeming hesitant to bring up the topic of my old boyfriend – who'd plunged a stake into the love of my life. "He…"

"He didn't really try to kill Lucius," I reassured her. "It was all a set up, to save Lucius's life, actually."

"Yeah, your mom told me the story," Mindy said. "There were so many rumors, and so much confusion after that night… I had to go ask her, one day, what was true."

"Lucius tried to invite Jake to the wedding," I added. "Even volunteered to fly him here. He feels so grateful for what Jake did."

Mindy's eyes widened with surprise. "And?"

I shook my head, before Mindy could start thinking anybody else from school would be at the ceremony. "He declined. I think he'd rather just forget the whole thing." Maybe forget me, too, after how I'd treated him.

"Yeah, I can see him wanting that," Mindy said. "Jake doesn't seem like a guy who'd like a fancy wedding – especially with vampires."

"No, I don't think he'd be comfortable in a castle," I agreed. Yet I still thought of Jake as a hero. A nice guy who'd tried to do the right thing. But I was destined for somebody very different. A prince who was probably at that very moment donning formal dinner attire, or running a razor over his jaw, being careful at the spot where his skin was scarred. Or maybe he'd be issuing last-minute orders to his staff, or pacing around his study, his hands laced behind his back as he prepared the toast he'd probably give that night.

Although I saw Lucius nearly every day now, my stomach started to tickle, like it always did when I thought of him, and I began moving us toward the SUV again, suddenly in a hurry. "Come on, let's go."

"Where's the dinner going to be, anyhow?" Mindy asked, following my lead.

The driver reached out and opened the door for both of us, and as I climbed in, I grinned over my shoulder. "Let's just say that in a few hours, you'll get a much closer look at Lucius's house!"

"Oh, boy," Mindy muttered, climbing in, too. "Oh, boy."

And for the second time that evening, I couldn't quite tell whether she was excited or scared. Or maybe I was projecting my own feelings again. For although I knew that Jake Zinn wasn't on the guest list, I wasn't exactly sure who all might show up.

CHAPTER 4

The Vladescu castle might have intimidated me with its sheer size and its grim history, and the stone walls could make it feel cold and formidable. But the dining room where Lucius and I held a pre-wedding dinner seemed warm and intimate as the people I loved most in the world gathered near the long, gleaming mahogany table, which reflected the light from no fewer than four massive wrought iron chandeliers, each one holding dozens of flickering tapers that cast a soft glow over the room.

Although we were both hosting the party, of course Lucius was there first – especially since my small group of guests was running late, thanks to Mindy's endless readjustment of both our hairstyles – and he smiled as we entered the room.

"Welcome, everyone," he greeted us, coming up beside me and slipping my hand into his. "You look beautiful tonight, Antanasia," he noted, glancing down to appraise the red dress I'd chosen for that evening. A long, full, silk gown with a delicate pattern of Swarovski crystals across the "bodice," as Lucius would say. I'd chosen the dress not really to impress him, but to honor my birth mother, who'd been known for wearing crimson.

"Red is a fitting color, tonight," Lucius added, like he recognized the tribute. Then he bent slightly, cupped my chin in his hand and kissed me. Even though I was about to be a wife, I was still a teenager, too, and I flushed a little, because my parents were right there. Not too long ago, I'd been humiliated just to be caught sitting on the porch with Lucius, both of us moving close to a kiss that never quite happened.

"I'm glad you like the gown," I told Lucius, fighting that urge to blush. "You look nice, too."

Then Lucius released my hand and stepped past me to greet my parents. "Ned, Dara – so nice to see you. Welcome to my home."

"It's good to see you, too, Lucius," Mom said, pulling him to herself and holding him tightly. "We've missed you."

In spite of the way things had ended in Pennsylvania, my mother had forged a bond with Lucius while he'd lived with us, and I knew that she was being sincere then. The fact that Lucius – who had grown up without a mother – didn't answer right away also made me think that he was truly glad to see her again, too. "Thank you for coming," he finally said, and although his voice was quiet, I was pretty sure it was thick with emotions that he was working hard to control.

When Mom released him, he straightened and moved to my father, and while I suspected that Dad, even more than Mom, had distrusted Lucius during those last few weeks that he'd lived with us, Ned Packwood was never one to turn away a hug. The two men hesitated for just a second, then Dad threw his arms wide and invited, "Come here, you!" Clasping Lucius to himself, he gave his back about five hearty slaps, until Lucius, laughing, withdrew and held Dad at arms' length, noting, "Easy, Ned! You strike hard for a pacifist!"

We all laughed, then, and all at once I exhaled with an audible whoosh and felt my shoulders relax. I hadn't even realized how tense I'd been about their meeting until I saw that things were fine between them.

I knew that my parents were still worried – maybe terrified – about me marrying into vampire royalty. But a part of them had always known that this moment might come, and, true to their beliefs about parenting, they were letting me be the adult they'd raised me to be, and accepting Lucius back. To be honest, I doubted they'd ever really let him go.

Then Lucius went to Mindy, who suddenly seemed uncertain about how to act in such a regal setting. Or maybe she was worried, in her own way, about reuniting with Lucius, after everything that had happened in high school. "Umm…" She actually started to curtsey and held out her hand, like she expected him to kiss it. But Lucius smoothly drew my friend into a less vigorous, but still welcoming, embrace. "Thank you, Melinda, for coming."

"I wouldn't have missed this for the world, Lukey," Mindy said, as they stepped apart. "I've been stocking up on shoes for this kind of shindig for years!"

It was probably the first time Lucius had ever been addressed by such a casual nickname in his own castle, but it seemed to amuse him – along with Mindy's first shoe reference of the trip. "Well, I hope the event is worthy of your footwear," he told her. Then he turned to me, saying, "I'm sorry, but I have to excuse myself. I need to 'mix and mingle' with our Romanian guests, as you Americans would say."

I looked around to realize that several other people – vampires – had arrived while we'd been preoccupied. Among them I saw some of my Dragomir kin, including my Uncle Dorin, whose face was already flushed with the warmth of the room and maybe the glass of dark red wine that he held in his hand as he told some animated story to three of my cousins.

I turned to look across the room, to a far corner, and saw that Lucius's Uncle Claudiu had joined us, too, and the peace that I'd just felt to see my friends and family reunited was shaken a little.

Claudiu – younger brother of Vasile, whom Lucius destroyed in this very house...

I hadn't been sure Claudiu would show up for a happy occasion. Although he was one of the Elders who ruled the clans, there was no love lost between him and Lucius. But Lucius, always one for decorum, had insisted that we invite him, because to do otherwise would alienate him further and maybe even cause a rift that couldn't be fixed.

Claudiu's presence in the room seemed to dim the candles a little, though. I stared at him, remembering that – along with eternal love – politics, intrigue and diplomacy were part of my new life, too. I'd be binding myself to whole the Vladescu clan when I said "I do" to the vampire who was pressing his palm against my back, promising me, "I won't be long, Antanasia."

"I'll go with you," I offered, thinking that it was probably proper for me to greet everybody.

But Lucius stopped me by moving his hand to my arm and giving it a reassuring squeeze. "You will have time to speak to everyone later," he said, with a smile. "Why don't you look after our American visitors? I can bring our relatives to you, which is perfectly fitting, given that you are not only royalty, but also – for one more day – still technically a guest here."

I gave him a grateful look, knowing that he was probably bending protocol a little to give Mom, Dad and especially Mindy time to settle in before they were left alone at a party where they were outsiders. I looked around the room once more, noting that more guests had arrived and trying to recall who was a Vladescu and who was a Dragomir. Not that I wasn't practically an outsider, myself.

Then I watched Lucius walk with his usual confidence toward Claudiu and the small group that surrounded Vasile's brother, and I envied my betrothed the ease with which he moved in the circles of power that I was joining.

I also found myself appreciating other things about Lucius. His always impressive height; his thick, black hair, cut a little bit shorter and neater than he normally wore it, for our wedding; and the way he carried off the dark, custom-tailored suit that he'd chosen for this occasion.

I was so caught up in observing him that I barely noticed Dad saying to Mindy, "Come on, Melinda Sue! Let's see if we can't find something to drink."

I probably should have offered to help them, but I was kind of transfixed to think that I was about to marry the guy who was smiling as he talked with his uncle, acting like there was no tension between them.

"Your prince looks very handsome tonight."

My mother whispered that in my ear, and I jolted, then turned to find her laughing at me, a teasing look in her eyes.

"Mom!" I started to protest. But there was really no reason to deny that I was admiring Lucius, like I used to do. "It seems like he's getting even more handsome, to me," I admitted.

I stole another look at Lucius and saw that he was still deep in conversation with his uncle – and still managing to grin.

"I think he's getting more handsome, too," Mom agreed.

I jerked back a little, surprised by the comment, only to see that she wasn't laughing anymore. "He's happy, Jessica. Happiness makes people beautiful."

I smiled at my mother. "I hope he's happy, Mom."

Then Dad and Mindy rejoined us, just in time for Lucius's deep voice to break into the quiet conversations that were taking place around us. "Please, everyone, take your places," he urged. "Dinner is served."

I went to my spot at one end of the table, Lucius took his at the distant other end, and the rest of the guests searched for their names on the vellum place cards that were artfully arranged on silver chargers before each tall chair.

As we all took our seats, I realized that there was one empty place – one person missing, at Lucius's right hand – and for the life of me, I couldn't recall who was meant to sit there.

I was distracted from wondering, though, as a team of silent, uniformed servers swept away the place cards and replaced them with individual menus explaining the night's selections in hand-printed, swirling calligraphy.

One by one, the menus were slipped beneath our noses.

And a few seconds later, all of us Americans began to laugh out loud.

CHAPTER 5

"That's a nice touch, you two," Dad said, grinning at me, then Lucius. "Very thoughtful!"

I smiled at Lucius, too. His secret, last-minute addition to the menu – "Lentil Casserole a la Vladescu" – was definitely an inside joke, given how he'd despised my parents' reliance on grains and beans, and especially lentils, but it was also just a nice thing to include for them.

"The casserole is Lucius's idea," I admitted, ignoring the confusion on my vampire relatives' faces. I was sure they all knew what lentils were, but their significance on the menu was going right over the Vladescus' and Dragomirs' heads.

Mom knew that Lucius was joking with her, though. He hadn't exactly been shy about sharing his opinions on her cooking in the past. "You should have called and asked for my personal recipe, Lucius," she teased. "I would've shared it!"

Even from far down the table, which was being circled by two servers filling long-stemmed glasses with red wine, I could see the amusement in Lucius's eyes. "Oh, I couldn't trouble you like that!" he joked. "Let's see how my cook handles this ever-so-adaptable and persistent little legume on her own. I am always eager to taste a new variation!"

All at once, to see Lucius at the head of that huge table, in control of the menu and the conversation, I was really struck by the magnitude and speed of the changes taking place in my life. Less than a year ago, Mom had practically dragged Lucius by the ear from our modest dining room table and scolded him for being rude to Jake during our first date. I looked from Mom to Lucius and back again, thinking that could never happen now. Lucius was far beyond anyone's control.

I was living independently in a new country, but was I a real adult like that, too?

14

I squirmed on my chair and glanced at Mindy, who was warily eyeing the almost dizzying array of silverware that was spread out before each of us. I wasn't sure if I knew when or how to use some of the gleaming implements, either.

I'd wielded power with Lucius on the night that I'd stopped the vampire war and claimed my place as leader of the Dragomir clan. But I couldn't help wondering in that moment... Who did I resemble more?

Lucius, at ease and in command?

Or Mindy, smiling – but nervously?

The two servants pouring wine reached Lucius and me at the same time, their performance choreographed to serve us last, and I nearly placed my hand over my glass to signal that I didn't want – couldn't drink – wine. Then I looked quickly to Lucius and saw that he seemed oblivious to being served. I glanced at my parents, too, as if for approval, before remembering that a sip of wine was legal for me in Europe, and I no longer needed permission. More to the point, I would be expected to take part in the toast, even if the taste made me cringe.

I slipped my hand back down to my side, hoping that nobody had noticed my near mistake and watching as the dark, almost black, liquid swirled into the glass. In the firelight, it looked a lot like something else that I wanted much, much more. Craved and needed, actually.

Then out of the corner of my eye, I saw Lucius rise, and my attention shifted back to him as he raised his own glass high to toast us all.

I knew that he was enjoying himself. That I was seeing Lucius Vladescu in his element. Yet I was also keenly aware that part of his enjoyment stemmed from the very fact that, given who was in the audience, even something as simple as welcoming guests could be fraught with peril. That one snub, intended, unintended or merely perceived, could have serious repercussions.

I looked around at my Dragomir relatives – and at Lucius's Uncle Claudiu, who sat stiffly in his seat, his long, pale fingers gliding up and down the stem of his wineglass – and my throat tightened.

Claudiu would probably love a war. As a Vladescu Elder, he'd been part of the plot to have Lucius dispose of me some dark night in the bed that we'd share, so the Vladescus could wield unchallenged power over an empire of vampires.

I turned back to Lucius, almost terrified, suddenly, by my own future, and desperate for reassurance that he really could keep me from harm. And seeing Lucius did calm me.

Still, my eyes darted back to Claudiu. But what about those times when Lucius couldn't be at my side?

I was so preoccupied with fighting a rising panic that it took me a second to notice that Lucius hadn't started his toast yet. Wasn't even looking at his guests – or me.

No, his attention was drawn to the wooden door at my back, which squeaked open on its old hinges. As the door swung wider, ushering in a chilly draft that made the candles flicker in the chandeliers, Lucius's expression changed dramatically, so I forgot all about Claudiu and secret plots.

I started to swivel around in my seat, certain that whoever was entering the room wasn't just some servant bearing another tray. And just as I twisted to see behind myself, Lucius confirmed my suspicions that somebody important had joined the party.

"Although he arrives deplorably behind schedule," Lucius announced, as I caught my first glimpse of the last, late-arriving guest, "I ask you all to welcome my one and only brother!"

CHAPTER 6

Brother?

For a split second the word caught me completely off guard, and I had this flash of betrayal, certain that Lucius had kept something important – a huge secret – from me. He didn't have a brother.

I was stunned, too, by our new guest's appearance as he sauntered into our midst, making a beeline for Lucius.

The rest of us were in formal attire. Even Dad, who usually wore decrepit t-shirts that advocated for causes no one had even thought about in ten years, was in a suit. But the guy who was strolling the length of the room, grinning like he didn't realize he was making a scene, had on a pair of grubby board shorts and a yellow t-shirt that advertised a Venice Beach surf shop.

As he passed by the table, the candlelight reflected off glossy, long brown hair that was cinched into a loose ponytail with what looked like an old leather shoelace. Hair that was maybe *too* glossy, like it needed a wash.

I also noticed a familiar sound as he walked, and glanced down at his feet, where I discovered a pair of black, rubber...

Flip flops?

I rose uncertainly from my seat and turned to Lucius, wanting some sort of explanation and – even in my shock – half expecting my impeccably mannered vampire prince to be very displeased. If this really was his brother, the late arrival... the sloppy clothes... they were disrespectful.

But when I saw Lucius's face, I realized that he didn't seem angry.

On the contrary, he was also grinning from ear-to-ear, setting down his glass and pushing aside his chair in order to step toward the newcomer.

What the...?

I looked at my parents and Mindy, who also seemed confused, and was embarrassed to be able to do nothing more than offer them a baffled shrug.

Still standing awkwardly, I spun back to Lucius just in time to see him extend a handshake to the guy he'd called brother, who in turn clasped my future husband's hand before pulling him into the same kind of back-slapping embrace that Lucius had just shared with my dad.

Then Lucius grabbed the stranger by the shoulders and spun him to face us, so I could see that they shared nearly identical smiles and the gleaming white teeth of Vladescu nobility. Only then did I realize who this person really was. It was almost like I was thinking the words that Lucius spoke when he announced, still smiling, "This surf bum who dares to join us – late – and in such inappropriate attire is, I am almost ashamed to admit, my best man."

I sank back down onto my seat, still not quite believing my eyes.

This… *this*… was the legendary Raniero Vladescu Lovato?

CHAPTER 7

"So…" Mindy drew her knees up to her chest and wrapped her arms around her legs, probably trying to keep warm in my bedroom, which was chilly even in summer. "What's up with that Raniero guy? He was a surprise, huh?"

I finished buttoning up my pajamas and crawled onto the mattress with her, like we were having one of our slumber parties back in Lebanon County. "Raniero's definitely not what I expected," I agreed.

Mindy cocked her head. "So what do you know about him?"

"Only that he's Lucius's cousin. But Lucius considers him a brother, because he spent a lot of time at the Vladescu estate when they were growing up. They were raised like siblings."

"Doesn't Raniero have parents, either?" Mindy asked, with sympathy in her voice. "Why'd he live with Lukey so much?"

I smiled at Mindy's use of that nickname again. I'd missed that, along with everything else about my best friend. "Raniero does have parents – in Italy," I explained, trying to recall everything that Lucius had told me about his best man. "But the Elders thought it would be wise to educate him with Lucius."

Mindy seemed confused, maybe because we'd grown up in a culture where "heirs to the throne" weren't such a big deal. "Why?" she asked.

"Since Lucius really is an only child, the Elders thought it would make sense to prepare another young Vladescu vampire to step in. Just in case something should happen…"

I couldn't bring myself to finish that sentence. Not on the eve of my wedding, when I was supposed to be planning for a long, happy future with Lucius. I couldn't even think about the possibility of something awful happening to him.

"Anyway, the Elders thought Raniero showed promise and could be

19

raised to serve as Lucius's right hand man, almost like a general," I added. "A second-in-command, since there's no pure-blooded Vladescu brother."

"So what went wrong?" Mindy asked, grabbing a pillow and hugging that to her chest, too. "Because Raniero doesn't look like he could lead a limbo contest at whatever beach he washed up on, let alone take charge of an army or a nation!"

I shrugged. "Lucius hasn't revealed much more about him. Only that he abruptly moved to California a few years ago, putting distance between himself and the clan leaders."

I wondered, suddenly, if Raniero had ever endured time in those dungeon rooms I'd seen. Or was that type of "education" reserved for genuine princes-in-training? Because if Raniero did bear some of the same scars Lucius did – if he'd been taken into those dark chambers to be "educated" to within an inch of his life – I could imagine why he'd gone to live on a beach in the sunshine.

"He and Lucius are obviously still close, though," I added, dismissing more awful thoughts. Memories of the way Lucius's uncles had thrashed him when they'd come to Pennsylvania, and how that had changed him, and taken him to a dark place.

"Well, Lucius and Raniero sure are different," Mindy noted, rolling her eyes. "Lucius is totally royal, and Raniero is, like, a slacker!"

Although my thoughts had just been trapped in a dismal dungeon, I couldn't help laughing at the idea of a slacker vampire – especially a Vladescu slacker. "We only saw him for a few hours," I reminded her. "Maybe he was just having a rough day."

"Or a rough year," Mindy said. "That guy needs a haircut – or at least a shower!"

"Mindy!" I started to protest, wanting to defend Lucius's best friend. But I found that I couldn't do it. Raniero Vladescu Lovato had seemed a little… scruffy. He'd slurped down his soup like a starving barbarian, slouched in his chair, and actually summoned a servant by waving his hand and calling out, in his Italian accent with a California surfer twist, "Dude. More lentils, *prego*."

I'd kept looking at Lucius, expecting him to cringe or maybe even suggest that Raniero watch his manners, but I'd seen nothing more than indulgent amusement in my fiance's eyes.

Who, exactly, was this guy Lucius called "brother?" Had he really left behind a life of wealth and power to *surf*?

"I guess we'll see if he cleans up for the wedding, huh?" I said, laughing off any vague suspicions I might've had. "I can't imagine that Lucius would let his best man – even a guy he considers a brother – wear board shorts at the ceremony."

Mindy hugged her pillow tighter and frowned. "Unless somebody does a real extreme makeover on that guy between now and tomorrow, I'm not getting my hopes up."

"Hopes?" I asked, not sure why Mindy cared about Raniero at all. I mean, it was my wedding. If Lucius's best man looked like he'd just rolled in with the tide, that was my problem.

"Well, I'm the one who has to spend the whole wedding with him, right?" she reminded me. "And I at least have to dance with him, don't I?"

I realized, then, that as maid of honor, Mindy probably considered Raniero her date for the evening. And maybe, just maybe, she'd hoped that the guy she'd be paired with might be… better. Or, given her old crush on "Lukey," a little bit like the groom, himself, even. "Oh, Mindy…"

I wanted to tell her that I was both sorry that Lucius's best man was a disappointment – and that she really wouldn't want to even think about getting involved with any vampire. I was born to marry Lucius – couldn't wait to do it – and yet I wouldn't necessarily recommend blood, eternity, and being considered frighteningly different as a lifestyle for any of my friends.

Before I could advise Mindy that she was probably lucky that Raniero wasn't her type, though, we were interrupted by a knock on the door, and my mom poking her head in to ask, "Mindy? Would you mind if I spoke to Jessica alone for a minute? I have something to give her."

I started to tell Mom that Mindy could probably stay. After all, we were practically sisters, as surely as Lucius and Raniero were brothers. But then I saw the look on Mom's face, and I turned to Mindy, telling her, "I think you'd better go, okay?"

Because the expression my mother was wearing… I hadn't seen her look like that in all the years she'd raised me.

CHAPTER 8

Mindy had obviously sensed my mom's mood, too, and she was already crawling off the bed, agreeing, "Sure, Dr. Packwood. I should go to my room anyhow. Tomorrow's a big day!"

When Mindy offered that reminder, my heart seized with anticipation – and fear again. I'd managed to distract myself from thoughts of the wedding for a few minutes, but in just hours I'd don my dress, and a servant would arrive with the things I'd need for a private act I'd have to perform first.

Will I have the nerve to do that?

"It's gonna be wonderful," Mindy reassured me, no doubt seeing the blood draining from my face. "I mean, you're getting married! To Lucius!"

Yes, I am. It's really happening.

Then she leaned in to give me a quick hug, said her goodnights, and left me and Mom alone.

I climbed off the bed, too, and walked toward my mother, curious about that look on her face, and an object that she held in her hands. "What is that?" I asked. "What's going on?"

Mom smiled, but that didn't quite erase the sad, almost solemn, look in her eyes as she said, "I have an early wedding gift for you. Something I want you to have tonight."

I looked again at the item she carried, thinking that the present was as strange as my mom's mood. Unlike most wedding gifts, this one wasn't wrapped in pretty paper. Rather, the package that Mom cradled with obvious care was covered by a plain white cloth, which she started to unwind, almost like a bandage.

"This is a special gift from both me – and your birth mother," Mom revealed, continuing to unwrap the object.

Even more intrigued, I came a little closer to her. "Mom?"

22

"I promised Mihaela that I'd give this to you on the eve of your wedding, if you married Lucius," she said. "Keep it safe, like Mihaela did, and then me, on your behalf. Because this, in turn, may keep *you* safe."

She looked up, and I saw that odd expression in her eyes again, and I understood, somehow, that Mom was, in that moment, giving me away. The ceremony tomorrow would be a formality to her. This act – whatever she was giving me – symbolized the completion of her pledge to raise me as her own, but for Lucius and the family that I was returning to.

"Mom…" I heard the fear in my voice. I wasn't ready and didn't want to leave *her*.

But of course my mother knew that I *was* ready, and that I had to leave my old life behind, and she held out the present, no longer covered, pressing it into my hands.

"You're going to be a wonderful ruler and a wonderful wife," she promised, her voice as close to shaky as I ever expected to hear it. "You and Lucius are two incredibly special individuals, and you share a very strong love. I knew that even before you both did."

Apparently Lucius and I had been the last to know.

Then, before I could really even see what she'd given me, Mom hugged me and whispered, "I'm proud that you're my daughter. And I'm so glad that Mihaela chose me to be your mother, too."

"You'll always be my mom," I said, hating that it sounded like we were saying good-bye.

"I know, Jessica… Antanasia," she corrected herself. "And you will always have a home in Pennsylvania. But I also know that your life is centered here now – and that it will be, long after your father and I are gone."

For the first time that I could remember, Dr. Dara Packwood seemed unable to come to grips with a concept – eternity, as it related to me – and we both fell silent, just holding each other.

"I love you, Jessica," she said, deciding to use my old name.

"I love you, too, Mom." She started to pull back, but I grabbed her wrist. "You'll help me get ready tomorrow, right?"

"Of course," she promised. "Of course!"

I felt relieved, because I'd almost been afraid that we really were separating from one another. And yet something had definitely shifted between us.

I wanted Mom to stay longer, but she left me then. And when the door closed behind her, I finally looked at the gift in my hands, and I thought it was appropriate that it had come wrapped in a cloth like a bandage, because it seemed like my heart cracked, just to hold something so precious.

And I wasn't sure whether I was addressing Dara or Mihaela – or maybe both of them – when I said, voice catching, "Oh, Mom…"

CHAPTER 9

"... trust your instincts – and distrust anyone who makes you the slightest bit wary, even among your closest 'friends.'"

"... Vladescus are strong willed, but a Dragomir princess never cowers..."

"I will always be a part of you, Antanasia..."

I closed the black, leather-bound notebook and sank down onto my bed, not even sure how I'd gotten back across the room, because I'd been so absorbed in reading my birth mother's cramped but careful script. It seemed as though she'd tried to fill every inch of the tiny booklet – small enough to be carried in a pocket, or maybe hidden in a fugitive child's blankets – with all of her collected wisdom. Everything that she'd obviously thought I would need to know to be the ruler of not one, but two, clans. And to be the wife of a "rival" prince.

I stroked the cover with my fingertips, overwhelmed by how much she must have loved me to have left me such a legacy.

Lucius had given me the manual for becoming a vampire; Mihaela Dragomir had provided me with the guide to surviving as one.

I closed my eyes for a moment, bowing my head in a gesture of gratitude and respect for her, too.

Thank you, Mihaela, for protecting me, even when you clearly saw your own destruction looming.

Although I'd only skimmed passages, knowing that I'd read more carefully in the months and years to follow, I'd seen how her messages had become clipped and her handwriting jagged as the pages ran out, like she'd known that the time for recording her thoughts was running low, too.

Shivering, suddenly realizing that the room had gotten even colder while I'd stood reading, I slipped between my blankets and tucked the little volume under my pillow, like maybe I could absorb her wisdom in my sleep. I also wanted to keep the notebook right with me. Even my nightstand seemed too far away for something so valuable.

Resting my head on my pillow, I closed my eyes, already feeling warmer, not just from the blankets, but because it felt like I had a new ally, who had already experienced the things that I faced, and who could help me.

I understood, then, why my adoptive mom had felt like she was handing me back to my birth mother when she'd given me the present.

Although the gift and the evening were bittersweet, I started to smile, remembering a specific passage that I'd noted as I'd paged quickly along.

"... hope that you come to love him..."

I knew that Mihaela referred to Lucius, who I had come to love, more than I ever could've dreamed when I'd struck his foot with a pitchfork, less than a year before.

Smiling in the dark, I started trying to picture our wedding. But maybe because I still wasn't sure where it would be held, I had trouble imagining it. And like often happened since the evening Lucius had proposed to me, I found myself remembering *that*. And even though I'd been sure I'd never fall asleep that night, before long I was drifting into my favorite dream, which always started with Lucius taking my hand and leading me down a secret path that only a handful of vampires – and two very special humans – even knew existed.

"Come with me, Antanasia," he invites, his fingers strong and cool around my hand. "It's time that I show you a place that is not just special, but sacred..."

CHAPTER 10

The path is steep, carving sharply up the mountainside, taking us higher than I've been in the Carpathians yet, and I cling tightly to Lucius's hand, getting short of breath even though we're walking slowly. The terrain is rockier here, and the trees have thinned out. The air, itself, is thinner, making the climb even more difficult.

Even Lucius, who's fit and was raised in these mountains, seems to breathe a little harder. It's getting dark and we aren't speaking, too busy concentrating on our footing, and in the silence I can hear him inhaling and exhaling in steady rhythm by my side.

And then the quiet of that lonely spot is broken by the sound of someone — something — close by, but hidden from sight. Footsteps moving quickly in the opposite direction, slipping and sliding down the mountain so rocks are dislodged and tumble toward the valley below.

Who or whatever has passed us sounds big. Or maybe there are more than one of them.

I crush Lucius's fingers with mine, pulling us both to a stop, and note in a whisper, with barely concealed alarm, "Lucius? It's getting late." I peer into the distance, looking for forms or shadows in the direction of that ominous rustling. "Do you think maybe we should come back tomorrow?"

I know that I don't need to remind him that there are bears and wolves — and people who destroy vampires — in these mountains. I'm sure that he'll understand why I'm getting nervous.

The sound of footsteps grows fainter, muffled by a rising wind, but I'm not reassured, until Lucius, who's been a half-step ahead, guiding us on a trail I've completely lost track of, turns and asks softly, "Would I let any harm come to you, Antanasia? Allow you even to stumble — until you know these paths by heart, yourself?"

As I try to meet his eyes in the gathering darkness, the wind rushes down the valley again, crashing into us, and I almost do lose my footing. And of course he's there to steady me, clasping my arm with his free hand.

I get my balance, but we stand there for a second face-to-face, and I forget about my fears, because like always happens when we're alone, I want to kiss him.

Far away, I hear more noise. In a split second, I want to go home again.

But Lucius has other plans – a destination – in mind.

"Come along," he says, starting to walk again. This time, our pace is even slower, because the terrain is getting even trickier and the air is getting very thin for lungs like mine, used to life near sea level in southern Pennsylvania.

My eyes are trained downward, and I'm so focused on picking my way through the rocks that I lose track of everything around me, including time, so I'm surprised when Lucius suddenly halts and squeezes my hand harder, signaling that I should stop walking and raise my face to look ahead.

And when I do, I am confronted by... nothing.

CHAPTER 11

Although he hasn't revealed our destination, I've known from the start of our adventure where Lucius is taking me. Still, the utter blackness in front of me – the tall, narrow hole like a slit into the side of the mountain – makes me pull back a little.

Lucius doesn't hesitate, though. Without a word, he steps inside first, and because our hands are linked – and because I want to follow – I let him guide me into the constricted passage, so small that Lucius has to walk ahead, slightly bent, his arm stretched behind himself to reach me. We move at a snail's pace, feeling our way along, because there's no hope of our eyes adjusting in such a complete subterranean void.

I want to ask him why we couldn't have brought a flashlight or a candle, even, but something tells me not to talk.

I'm scared. Scared of being in a tight space underground, in darkness that almost certainly hides creatures that would make my skin crawl if I could see them. And I have irrational fears, too, like that the ground might drop away and our next step send us tumbling into empty space. But I'm also excited and know that Lucius is familiar with the tunnel.

As if on cue, he turns – not easy in the cramped space – and rests his free hand gently on my head, protecting it as he guides me past a turn where stone juts down from above. "Careful here," he whispers. "The rock is sharp."

Yes, it's quite obvious that Lucius has been here many times.

As I round the bend, ducking low, I see a faint glow in the distance, and my anticipation grows, along with a new confusion.

Is someone else already here? Are we meeting somebody?

If Lucius is surprised, he doesn't voice it. He just continues to draw us down the curving corridor and toward that light, and my eyes finally begin to pick out details around us. The passageway is actually very dry and smooth, not as scary as I'd thought in the dark. The walls appear almost cared for. I glance down and see that the dirt floor seems swept clean, too. And the air, though musty, smells like spice. Maybe some kind of incense. I take a deep breath, thinking the smell is vaguely reminiscent of the unusual cologne that I first began to associate with Lucius back in America.

I walk close on his heels, wondering if Lucius chose that cologne because it reminded him of this spot.

The light grows stronger, and my heart starts to pound. I am about to see what is probably – no, definitely – the most significant place in my life.

We take a few steps more, and the ceiling rises higher, so even Lucius can stand upright, and at the last moment – just as we pass under a crude wooden support that separates the passage from the chamber that lies at the end – he draws me to his side and then steps aside, allowing me to walk through first and telling me, his voice hushed with reverence, "This, Antanasia, is where our parents promised us to one another."

As I step into that hidden cavern, lit by a row of simple candles arranged on a wooden table, almost like an altar… That honestly is the first time it really strikes me that I've been here before. That the infant I sometimes picture being offered up at a underground betrothal ceremony was actually ME.

That child always seemed like a stranger. No more real than a doll.

But of course that baby was… me. My eyes have witnessed all of this before. Maybe I was placed on that table.

And Lucius…

I turn slowly to face him and see that he looks both happy and suitably solemn, clearly understanding what is running through my mind. "Yes, Antanasia," he says. "This – THIS place – is where you and I REALLY first met."

He stays near the entrance, giving me time to take everything in.

The cave isn't large, but like the tunnel, it's clean and obviously maintained. Along with the table, there are wooden benches arranged in rows, almost like a classroom or a church.

"This is where our ancestors made all of their most important decisions," Lucius explains. "The Elders and senior vampires would gather here to debate. Still do gather, for the most crucial, clandestine meetings."

I look at him and see that his gaze is traveling around the space, like he's seeing it anew, too.

"And they sought refuge here, too, right?" I ask. "When vampires were being purged?" A chill runs through me – and not because the cave is cool. Our parents were destroyed in the last purge. Will there be others?

"Yes," Lucius answers my spoken questions. "This has always been a safe haven. Its location is highly guarded." He meets my eyes, adding, "Destruction awaits the vampire who reveals this spot to a human. That is the penalty, with no hope of clemency. No mercy."

I know that's not exactly true. "But what about my parents? They were here."

"The fact that an exception was made for your mother and father speaks to the trust that our clans placed in them. I believe that the Vladescus and Dragomirs hoped that your mother's work would help the world to understand our culture better." Lucius's mouth sets in a grim line. "But such was not the case. And since the purge, the penalty

for revealing this spot is once again destruction. With no exceptions."

I watch Lucius coolly stating this fact, and although I know that he's prepared to rule, I'm a little bit in awe — and slightly unnerved — to think that the vampire who just protected my head with a gentle hand wouldn't hesitate to carry out that kind of justice.

Uncertainty grips me. Will I, as a princess, really be responsible for handing down such a sentence? Am I responsible for doing it NOW, if a Dragomir breaks the code of secrecy?

I stare hard into Lucius's eyes. Has he already served as judge, issued a decree like that?

I start to ask him, but change my mind. Maybe I don't want to know. Not right then. So I ask another question that's bothering me. "If this is a safe haven, why didn't our parents...?"

But Lucius is already shaking his head. "Rulers do not 'hide,' Antanasia," he reminds me. "Especially not leaders such as our parents were. Such as WE will be. Kings and queens do not cower in caves, even to save their existences."

I swallow thickly, a queer feeling in the pit of my stomach, and not only because I doubt my courage in the face of destruction. Lucius has also just elevated us to "king and queen." But he and I are barely a prince and princess. At least, I'm barely a princess. And to rise up to be queen requires a vote of confidence by all the clan members.

My concerns must be plain on my face, because Lucius steps closer to me, smiling in a reassuring way. "Don't look so alarmed, Antanasia." He takes my hands in his and bends to rest his forehead against mine. "Nothing bad is happening tonight!"

As we stand together in the quiet cave, the worry that I did feel dissipates. "I'm not scared," I promise him.

"Good." He clasps my hands together and presses them against his chest, so I can feel his heartbeat. "Because the last thing I want you to feel right now is fear."

After a few seconds, I realize that Lucius's heart is beating a little more quickly than usual. Just slightly faster and harder than its familiar slow, almost imperceptible pace, and I raise my face to his, wondering what's causing the change.

I see, then, that there's something different in his eyes, too. A flicker that tells me something is happening. Something more than just Lucius showing me the cave where generations of Romanian vampires have come to seal pacts and forge treaties and sometimes hide from persecution by humans.

Out of the corner of my eye, I catch sight of the candles flickering, too, and I have my second revelation of the evening.

Not only have I really been here before, but Lucius has prepared this spot for us this night.

The footsteps scrambling down the mountain... That was almost certainly one of his two guards, returning after getting the cave ready for our arrival.

And the fact that we've made this journey in the dark, when it would have been so much easier in daylight...

I study Lucius's dark eyes, wishing more than ever that I could read his thoughts as well as he seems able to read mine. "Lucius?" I ask him. "Why are we really here

tonight?"
    And his answer isn't at all what I expect.

CHAPTER 12

Lucius pulls back from me, just a step, but he continues to hold both of my hands in his, and his eyes are boring into mine. And gradually I see them change again.

Lucius has told me, many times, that he loves me. And I've seen that expressed in his eyes. But never like this. "I've brought you here this evening to ask you to marry me, Antanasia," he finally says. "I wanted to do it in this place, so significant to both of us."

All at once, everything – including time – seems to stop.

"Lu... Lucius..." I stammer his name, not sure I've heard right. Marriage to Lucius – both avoiding it and desperately desiring it – is practically all that I've thought about since meeting him and learning of the pact. I know that it's definitely in our future. And yet I still can't believe my ears, and I keep searching his face, almost like I'm afraid he's joking. "Lucius?"

For once, though, there's no mischief in his expression. Not a trace.

He squeezes my hands more tightly, pressing them harder to his chest. "I want to ask you, Antanasia – in this place where we were promised to one another by mandate – to marry me not because doing so is required of you, but because you love me as I love you," he says. "I ask you to choose me of your own free will, because that is how I choose you. Not to fulfill a pact, but to follow my heart, which will settle for nothing less than a life with you by my side."

I want to scream, "Yes!" I want to cry out and hurl myself into his arms. But my feet seem rooted in place, and my tongue is locked in my mouth.

And then – standing before me as an equal, which seems right for Lucius and me – better than having him drop down on bended knee – he poses the question I've wanted to hear, maybe since the day I first saw him.

"Antanasia, will you marry me?" He releases one of my hands to push my curls away from my face, and his voice is softer when he asks again, "Will you do me the honor of being my wife?"

That rare vulnerability I've just seen in Lucius's eyes is echoed in his voice, and it's that sweetness – that unguarded, hopeful request – that finally lets me speak. Because I know that this is the closest that Lucius will ever come to pleading for anything in his entire existence, and he's doing it for me.

"Yes, Lucius," I cry. At least, I think I cry out. But in truth, my voice is soft, almost choked. "Yes," I repeat, pulling my hands from his and wrapping my arms around his neck. I know he's heard me, but I keep agreeing, over and over again. "Yes, yes, yes."

He clasps me to himself, whispering in my ear, too. "Thank you, Antanasia. Thank you for loving me and for choosing me, too."

We hold each other for a long time as reality sets in. We're getting married, not to fulfill a treaty but because we can't exist without each other.

Then Lucius slips one hand up into my hair, and I shift in his arms to see his face again just before he bends to meet my lips with his, kissing me softly. We kiss like that again and again, just gently. It's like we both recognize that the moment deserves reverence, just like the space in which it takes place.

And somehow, while we're still kissing, Lucius takes my left hand and places a ring on my finger. I never even notice him reaching into his pocket and have no idea how long he's held the object in his palm.

I know that most girls would probably squeal and pull back, wanting to see the diamond, but I never even open my eyes. I just slip my arms back up around his neck, not caring what the ring looks like. I'm perfectly content with what we're sharing right then...

"Antanasia."

The voice intruded on my dream, and I rolled sideways, shutting it out, not wanting to leave behind everything that I was reliving. But the voice – Mom's voice – interrupted again, and I felt pressure on my shoulder as she shook me. "Antanasia!"

"Mom," I groaned, wanting five more minutes of the dream. "Please..."

But my mother shook me harder, and as I reluctantly opened my eyes, I heard her laughing at me.

I blinked about three times, because sunlight was streaming into my room and glinting off the huge, sparkling diamond that was always on my left hand now. A Vladescu family heirloom, which had been removed and hidden by Lucius's mother, Reveka, when she'd faced her destruction.

Then I looked at Mom, who seemed happy again. And maybe a little surprised to hear herself say words that kind of shocked me, too, even though I'd been planning, anticipating – and occasionally worrying about – this day for weeks.

"Wake up, sleepyhead," she urged. "You're getting married today!"

CHAPTER 13

I kept my back to the full-length mirror as I stepped into my wedding gown.

I wasn't sure if I wanted to surprise myself when I saw the full effect of the dress and the makeup that Mindy had done for me, and the intricate updo with the delicate tiara sparkling against my dark curls – or if I was afraid to look at my reflection and realize that the gown... that *I*... wasn't as beautiful as I'd hoped.

"Are you sure you don't want help?" Mindy called through the door that linked the two rooms of the suite that had been designated for my wedding preparations at the Vladescu estate. "I am your maid of honor!"

"No, it's okay," I told her. "I'll be right out."

Tugging the heavy, white silk up around my body, I held the dress in place with one hand while I reached around myself to pull up the hidden zipper. When I couldn't reach farther, I started to smile, remembering how Lucius had once surprised me by zipping up a similar dress for me, back in a Lancaster County shop. I'd started to see him – and myself – in a new way, that day.

"Jess, we're dying out here!" Mindy called, sounding eager and impatient. "Hurry up!"

"I'm hurrying," I promised, grinning at Mindy's enthusiasm, too. But I still took a second to smooth the fabric before finally turning to look in the mirror.

And the person I saw reflected there...

Wow.

CHAPTER 14

"Wow." Mindy spoke my thought aloud, practically skidding to a stop after bursting through the door. She paused, just staring, then came closer, walking slowly, like she was in awe of the dress. Or maybe she was in awe of *me*. Maybe, for the first time, she really saw me as a princess, because I felt like one. *Stood* like one. "Wow," she repeated, coming up next to me, so we could both check my reflection in the mirror.

Mom joined us, too, stepping up behind me and placing her hands on my bare shoulders. I saw that she also thought I looked beautiful. Different. "You are going to take Lucius's breath away," she promised.

I didn't say anything, because I didn't want to sound vain. How could I explain that I knew I wasn't a "pretty" girl, but that in that moment, I felt like the most beautiful bride on the face of the earth?

The top of the dress fit me like a glove, accentuating the curves that Lucius had helped me to embrace, before sweeping away into a full, snow-white train. But the bodice wasn't pure white, like a traditional gown. It was overlaid with black silk so delicate that it created an effect like a dove-gray mist swirling around me.

That detail, alone, might have been enough to make my wedding dress unconventional. But I'd wanted more than just something different. I'd wanted a dress that spoke to who I'd been in the past – that teenage girl – and also the ruler I was becoming. And so I'd instructed the tailor to add a cascade of black, hand-beaded lace flowers and leaves, twining like a wild vine across my body. It was a dark, dramatic touch that symbolized, to me, what Lucius called the "dark side of nature," which I'd joined when he'd first made me a vampire.

In the mirror, I met my own eyes – dark and dramatic, too, thanks to Mindy – and I believed that my mom might just be right. I really might take

Lucius's breath away, like I hoped.

The mirror also reflected a window across the room, and I noticed that the sun was going down. Vampires might already be gathering in whatever secret place Lucius had picked for the ceremony. And I was almost ready, except for one final act.

All at once, there was a knock on the door that led to the hallway, and, forgetting my dress – and that Mom and Mindy were there to do things like handle visitors – I hurried to answer it.

Swinging open the door, I found the person I'd expected waiting for me. My throat suddenly got a little dry, but I nodded for him to come in, knowing that the servant wouldn't really need any instructions.

And sure enough, he walked directly to a small table and set down the silver tray he carried.

Then, still without saying a word, he retreated to wait outside while I performed the first ritual of my wedding. The one that scared me most.

CHAPTER 15

I stood before the table, studying the objects on the tray. There was a small, silver, lidded cup, etched with a pattern of vines that had darkened over generations, the tarnish so black that obviously even polish couldn't remove it. The design reminded me of the vine that twined across my gown, making me even more glad that I'd chosen that detail. It almost seemed like, when I'd dreamed up my dress, I'd somehow connected to my mother, and her mother, and all of the Dragomir women who'd used this vessel before me, over the course of hundreds of years.

And my ancestors had also used the silver knife that was set next to the cup. And the spoon that held the pungent herbs, and the strips of bleached, cotton cloth folded under the blade...

Mom placed her hands on my shoulders again. I hadn't even realized that she and Mindy had joined me at the table. I twisted a little to see her face. "Mom?"

I wasn't sure what I wanted to ask, though. I knew what I had to do.

Mom gave me a reassuring smile, and I drew some strength from how calm she looked. "You're going to be fine," she promised. Then she turned me so we were facing each other and pulled me to herself, squeezing me tightly. "I'm going to join the other guests now," she said, stepping back.

"No." I clutched at her hands. "Don't go yet!"

I wanted her to help me, but she shook her head. "No, Antanasia. It's time for me to go."

I knew my mother well enough to understand that she had deliberately chosen this moment to leave. She'd also purposely used my new name again. My wedding was starting, and I would have a lot of difficult things to deal with in the future, without her by my side. It was time for me to start facing them.

"I know it's hard, but try not to be scared," Mom added one last piece of advice. "You want to savor every moment of this night. It's not about getting everything right. It's about you and Lucius promising yourselves to each other. That's all that matters."

I took a deep breath, then agreed, "I know."

"I love you," she said, hugging me one more time.

"I love you, too."

Then Mom left Mindy and me without another word, because we'd said all the important things the night before.

When the door closed behind my mother, Mindy looked at me with wide, nervous eyes, like she wished that calm, competent Dr. Dara Packwood was still with us, too. "Um, what do I do, Jess?" she asked, her eyes darting to look at the tray. "Do I... help you?"

I shook my head. "No. Just stay in the room in case something goes wrong."

My maid of honor got a little pale, but she nodded. "Okay."

Then Mindy, seeming to sense that I needed some space, took a few steps back, and I sat down at the table. Without giving myself any more time to hesitate, I next stretched my right arm across the tray and used my left hand to lift the knife.

CHAPTER 16

Just as I placed the blade against my wrist, though, I stopped.

Cutting myself was going to hurt, and if the knife went too deep, I could find myself bleeding too much. People committed suicide by slitting their wrists.

I knew that I wouldn't really die that night – couldn't be destroyed that way – but I still found my fingers shaking as I rested the blade against a spot where a blue vein was visible just under the surface of my skin.

It was one thing to have Lucius gently pierce my flesh in a moment of passion, and quite another to sit there alone, like an untrained surgeon, and draw my own blood. Enough to fill a cup that suddenly seemed much larger than it had just moments before.

Behind me, Mindy shifted, and I knew that I needed to hurry. It was getting late, and I didn't want to keep our guests – and especially Lucius – waiting.

Lucius.

Somewhere in the recesses of the Vladescu estate, wherever he was getting ready, he would be performing the same ritual as me. I knew that his hand wouldn't be shaky, though. I could imagine him calmly lifting the knife, placing the blade against his flesh and drawing an almost invisible line down his arm. A line that would in seconds turn red as the blood began to flow out. Then he would turn his wrist over the cup and allow it to collect the drops.

My fingers more sure, I pressed my own knife harder against my skin, but I still flinched when the blade, as sharp as a real scalpel, broke through. I applied just a little more pressure and heard Mindy gasp as dark, thick liquid suddenly rushed out of the wound.

The narrow gash hadn't hurt at first, but it started to sting, then, and I sucked in a breath.

Just keep going, Jess. The worst part is over.

Steeling myself, I drew the blade about a half inch farther down my arm, then quickly turned my wrist so the blood that was coming faster, by then, dripped into the waiting cup.

I knew that Mindy was probably horrified – maybe even a little queasy – to watch me. If I had been in her shoes, I would've felt the same way. But of course, I'd changed, and I couldn't stop thinking that, in spite of the pain, the tradition had a certain beauty. It would give me and Lucius a way to share blood at the ceremony without biting each other's throats, which was, as Lucius had told me months ago, a very private act.

"Jess?" Mindy's uncertain voice broke into my thoughts, and I glanced up to find that she'd come close and was bending down beside me, a worried look in her eyes. "I think that's enough," she said, looking at my arm. "I think you should stop."

"Yes," I agreed, noting that the cup already held a few ounces. "That's enough."

I shifted and moved my arm so it lay flat on the tray, then used my other hand to lift the spoon full of herbs – willow and ginger – that would keep the blood from clotting too quickly. I stirred those into the cup, then started to reach for one of the pieces of cut cloth.

"Here." Mindy surprised me by taking my wrist in her hand and grabbing the cloth before I could get it. "Let me help, so you don't get blood on your dress."

"Okay," I agreed, letting her press the material against the wound.

After about a minute, Mindy carefully lifted a corner and peeked under. "I think it's stopped," she said. She met my eyes. "But I'll leave that piece on your arm, so we don't accidentally open the cut again, okay?"

I nodded. "Thanks." It wasn't exactly the right answer to Mindy's question, but I wanted her to know that I appreciated the calm, capable way she was dealing with a situation that most bridesmaids weren't asked to handle.

Then I watched as she wound a bandage around my arm with the same care she'd used when arranging my hair, and I knew without a doubt that I'd chosen the right person to be my maid of honor. That I'd chosen the right girl to be my best friend, years before.

"Thanks," I repeated, as she tucked away the tail of the cloth, so it looked as neat as possible.

When Mindy stood up, I raised my arm, thinking that the bandage, which I'd worried would mess up my appearance, was actually strangely right. And Lucius would have a nearly identical one, tied on by Raniero.

"Should I take this out?" Mindy offered, reaching for the tray.

"No, wait." I stopped her with a hand on her arm. "I'm not done yet."

"No?" Mindy's raised eyebrows and the way she kind of yelped told me that, while she was doing a great job coping with a vampire wedding, she'd seen me shed enough blood for one night.

But I had no choice, and I took the knife again, not scared this time, because I knew I could handle the sting. Using my left hand, I marked the palm of my right with a deep "x." Once again, the blood seeped out, and I picked up the last clean cloth, grasping it tightly in my fist to staunch the flow.

"Lucius will mark his left hand," I told Mindy, who seemed understandably confused. "So when we hold hands at the ceremony to speak our vows, our blood will be blended, palm to palm."

"Oh, wow." I could tell that Mindy, always a romantic, was torn between thinking that this was the most beautiful gesture ever, and believing that it was also totally wrong.

"Some vampires bear the scar for the rest of their lives," I added. "Like a wedding ring that you can't ever remove."

That was why I'd tried to cut my palm deeply. I wanted that permanent reminder of the night I married Lucius. I knew that Lucius would definitely make his cut deep, too.

Mindy didn't seem to know what to say to this, so I nodded to signal that it was time for her to take away the tray – and to stop worrying about whether I would use the knife again. "I'm done now, thanks."

"Okay." She put the lid on the cup and carried away the tray, balancing it with one hand when she opened the door.

The silent, waiting servant accepted the burden, and Mindy closed the door. As she came back across the room, she asked, "Now what?"

"We wait," I said, "for whoever will lead us to the wedding."

Once again, in spite of Mom's advice, the butterflies in my stomach started fluttering like crazy. Somewhere in the estate, our guests – vampire and human – would be assembled, and Lucius would be making his way to the ceremony.

But who was coming for me?

Another servant? One of Lucius's two guards?

I didn't have long to wonder, because before Mindy could even decide whether to risk wrinkling her dress by sitting down, there was another knock on the door, and I again rushed to answer it, too nervous and impatient to let my maid of honor do it.

And this time, when I opened the door to reveal the corridor, I saw that someone had been very, very busy while I'd been getting ready. I also greeted, with great happiness, my escort.

CHAPTER 17

"You look beautiful," Dad said, his eyes getting moist as he stepped into the room to greet us. But he was smiling, too. "Both of you!"

I saw that he took note of my bandage and the cloth that I was clutching in my hand, and a shadow crossed his face. I knew that, having traveled to Romania with Mom when she'd studied vampire culture, he would be familiar with the marriage rituals. And I had a feeling that, while he was always open-minded, he still didn't like seeing his own child bleed. But he didn't say a word.

Like Mom, he was letting go.

"You look pretty spiffy, yourself, Mr. Packwood," Mindy noted.

I checked out Dad's appearance, too, appraising him head to toe. When I got to the tips of his polished shoes, I raised my face to his and heard the surprise in my voice as I asked, "Dad?"

I'd expected my father to dress up for my wedding, but the tux he wore appeared custom fitted, not like some rental dragged from Pennsylvania in a garment bag. It rested perfectly on his shoulders and the pants broke just where they should, at the tops of those gleaming shoes. He'd donned a bow tie, too, and not only was it tied neatly, but it looked like somebody had checked it with a level.

In short, my dad seemed pretty regal, himself.

"It is my daughter's wedding," Dad reminded me, clearly understanding my shock. "Of course I'm wearing a tuxedo!" Then he grinned and noted, "Although, I'll admit that it's a very nice tuxedo, commissioned by Lucius, who apparently has some sort of issue with rented clothes."

I started laughing when Dad added, mimicking Lucius, "I have come to understand your passion for recycling, Ned, but I must draw the line at pants. Especially at my marriage!"

"Sounds like Lukey," Mindy agreed.

Then my father held out his arm for me, his elbow crooked, and offered, "Shall we? Your guests – and your groom – await the princess!"

Although the gesture was also kind of teasing – a fancy flourish to go with his suit – we both got serious. In a heartbeat, all of the laughter stopped.

Mindy sensed the mood change, too, and wordlessly stepped behind me as I took Dad's arm. I waited while she gathered up my train so it wouldn't drag along the floor when we walked to wherever the ceremony would be held.

It's really time, Jess.

"Dad," I said quietly, just before we stepped toward the door. "Do you know where we're going? This castle is like a maze!" I didn't want my father to give away Lucius's surprise location – not when I'd waited so long in suspense – but I was honestly worried about getting lost.

"Don't worry," he said. "We'll be fine."

Then he reached out to open the door, and as he ushered me through, I got the full view of something I'd only glimpsed when my father had slipped into the room, maybe purposely keeping me from looking down the hallway.

"Oh, it's beautiful," I gasped, stopping short.

Or maybe Mindy said that. Maybe we both did.

The entire corridor was lined with hundreds of flickering votive candles in small, leaded-glass holders. They were each about a footstep apart, providing the only light in the otherwise dark hallway.

Taking a deep breath, I squeezed Dad's arm, signaling that we should go, so the three of us began to follow that glowing trail.

We walked in silence for what seemed like a long time, heading into parts of the castle that I swore I couldn't recall seeing before. Or maybe Lucius had shown these places to me, and I couldn't remember them. Everything seemed different that night.

My heart, which had slowed when I'd become fully a vampire, started beating harder with each step. Yet I was getting strangely calm, too.

Lucius – my future – is waiting at the end of this path. This is the moment our parents planned for when they signed that scroll, eighteen years ago.

Ahead of us, I saw a bend in the corridor that was so sharp that for a second it looked like Mindy, my father and I were headed toward a dead end. And when we made the turn, I felt a warm breeze on my face and smelled fresh air, scented with flowers. A few yards away, the candles stopped at a curved archway cut into the stone wall.

I stole a look at Dad's face and saw that he was smiling again, like he knew what I was about to see.

And as we stepped under the arch, Mindy released the hem of my gown, letting it fall to the floor, while I pressed my hand against my chest, forgetting that I might stain my dress with blood from my palm, because my groom...

He had definitely outdone himself for me.

CHAPTER 18

Lucius had chosen for us to get married not in some grand ballroom, like I'd guessed, but in a small courtyard, like a grotto, that was bounded by stone walls smothered under creeping vines and twisting tendrils of moonflower, which snaked all the way up to the high eaves.

The only light came from the moon and even more candles, which were tucked into the sills of tall, arched windows that lined the walls and clustered by the dozens on a stone table where the small silver cups waited.

The whole scene was perfect, like Lucius had promised. Although we were at the center of a castle that he maintained with an eye for order and precision, the courtyard had a chaotic beauty. It sort of reminded me of my love for Lucius, which was like this out-of-control place at the center of *me*, who'd once insisted on rational, mathematical order, too.

Yes, that garden definitely caused me to draw a sharp breath.

But it was the sight of the vampire I was about to marry, not the amazing setting he'd created for us, that made me break protocol and say his name. "Lucius."

He stood waiting for me at the end of a path through the foliage, before the stone table, and I'd never seen him look so serious. But this wasn't the dark side of Lucius that sometimes came over him. I knew that he, even more than me, was thinking not only about our future together, as individuals who loved each other, but about history, and the fulfillment of that pact our parents had signed to unite our clans.

Although I was aware that our guests were waiting on rows of wooden chairs, I didn't walk toward him right away. We just stood for a second, sort of capturing the moment. I knew from his expression that he'd never forget how I'd looked when I entered the garden, just like I'd never forget the sight of him standing with his usual confidence, his broad shoulders drawn back and his hands clasped behind his back. A pose that was familiar to me.

But that night, Lucius didn't bow his head and pace. He stood perfectly still, his eyes fixed on me as we shared a very deep happiness that I also wanted to remember for the eternity that I hoped lay before us.

We might've stood like that for hours if Dad hadn't taken his arm from mine and kissed my cheek. I finally broke my gaze with Lucius to turn to my father, whose eyes glistened with tears again as he told me, "I love you, Jess."

I wanted to tell Dad that I loved him, too, but my throat suddenly caught. I knew he got what I wanted to say, though.

Then he stepped aside, because the tradition was for me to walk the final few feet alone. I didn't even carry flowers. I was supposed to approach Lucius empty handed, to symbolize that from that night on, there wouldn't be anything between us.

I nodded to Mindy, who stepped ahead of me and began to walk slowly down the pathway, and when she reached the end and took her place by the table, the guests stood up and turned, too. But I still barely noticed them, or Mindy, or Raniero standing at Lucius's left hand. I was again almost transfixed by the sight of my soon-to-be husband.

His black hair gleamed in the moonlight, which, together with the candles, illuminated his features, too. The high cheekbones, straight nose and strong jaw that I'd first noticed back in a Pennsylvania high school, a place that seemed a million miles from where we stood then. He wore a tuxedo that fit – and suited – him as perfectly as the garden fit our ceremony. The suit was understated – no tails or shiny silk lapels – but its simplicity only seemed to emphasize Lucius's self-assurance, like he didn't need flashy clothes to prove that he was a prince. Somehow, he managed to look like royalty in nothing more than an impeccably fitted dark coat, white shirt, black tie, and black pants.

He stood straight but at ease, like the warrior he'd also been raised to be, and I could hardly believe he was mine. I was pretty sure he was feeling the same way about me.

As I began to walk toward him, he pulled his hands from behind his back, reaching for me, and I saw a flash of white on his arm. The bleached cloth that peeked out from under his sleeve, just above his hand.

"Antanasia," he said, when I was close enough to hear him whisper. But he couldn't seem to say anything else. Had I actually rendered Lucius Vladescu speechless, maybe for the first time in his life? "I... I..."

I did smile, then, because I knew that I'd succeeded in taking his breath away, like I'd hoped.

I took my place next to him, and Lucius smiled, too. Holding out his left hand – the one he'd scored – he clasped my similarly marked right hand, squeezing our palms together, both to join us and to reopen the wounds we'd just made, so our blood could combine.

The incision on my hand stung again, and Lucius seemed apologetic about having to hurt me. I shook my head, though, trying to tell him that it was okay. Then we twisted our palms slightly, so our blood was definitely shared, like was supposed to happen.

We stood that way for a long moment, because this part of the ceremony was so important to vampires, until Lucius squeezed my hand again in a different way, and we turned to face the eldest of the Elders, who had joined us at the stone table, and who announced, "Let us begin."

CHAPTER 19

As our guests took their seats again behind us, Alexandru Vladescu, the ancient vampire presiding over our ceremony, reached across the table and rested his hands on both our foreheads, compelling me and Lucius to bow slightly while he offered our families' equivalent of a benediction.

"We gather this evening to unite, for eternity, Prince Lucius Vladescu and Princess Antanasia Dragomir, and to offer them the blessing of our clans," he said, his fingers firm against my head. "From this day forward, as promised in the pact sealed at their births, they shall live – and rule – as one."

Then he took away his hands, so Lucius and I could straighten, and I knew that I'd just witnessed one of only two times Lucius Vladescu would ever bow down before another vampire, no matter how venerable or powerful that Elder might be. The next time Lucius lowered his head would be at our coronation. If that day ever came.

I shifted my eyes slightly to see Lucius in profile. *Would he ever really be king? And could I really be QUEEN?*

"But first," Alexandru said, summoning my attention forward, so I found myself looking into eyes that were familiarly dark. Vladescu eyes, which had seen centuries, maybe millennia, of marriages, births – and destructions. "First you must accept one another as bride and groom, before your witnesses."

I clasped Lucius's hand more firmly and got a little nervous again.

Although I knew Lucius wanted to marry me, the question that was about to be asked wasn't just a formality, like in a regular wedding. In the world that I was entering, where unions really were eternal, the words that would be spoken next were meant to give both partners one last chance to reconsider before the die was cast forever.

"Lucius Vladescu," Alexandru said, his voice low, almost ominous, "will you accept Antanasia as your wife, now and always, for as long as you shall exist?"

Lucius and I turned to each another, and he took both my hands, and the moment that I saw his face, my apprehension vanished. "Yes," Lucius said, addressing everybody, but really talking only to me. "I accept Antanasia as my wife, now and always, for as long as I shall exist."

Although I'd known in my heart that Lucius would accept me, and that my momentary fear had been unreasonable, I was still relieved to hear him say those words out loud.

Then, while Lucius and I remained facing each other, Alexandru Vladescu spoke my name and asked me the same question. "Antanasia Dragomir, will you accept Lucius as your husband, now and always, for as long as you shall exist?"

I opened my mouth to answer, hardly even waiting for the elder vampire to finish. But just before the words came out of my mouth, Lucius whispered, "Antanasia. Wait."

CHAPTER 20

For a split second, I thought that Lucius had changed his mind about our marriage, and I felt all of my blood draining away. But when he lowered his eyes, concealing them from me, then raised them again, I realized that he was actually giving *me* one last chance to back out. In the last moments before I committed myself to Lucius forever, he let me see that dark, damaged place inside of himself that had driven him to press a sharpened stake against my chest, then break down and cry out, "Everything around me is destroyed!"

We were in public, and he couldn't say anything. But I knew what he was doing: Reminding me, one final time, that I was about to enter a very different, sometimes violent, culture, for good, with a vampire who'd once promised that he'd always be "treacherous."

There was no way our guests could have had any idea what was passing between us as we stood there, just staring into each other's eyes. They probably wondered if I was about to call off the wedding. Claudiu, at least, no doubt hoped that was happening.

He wouldn't get his wish.

Without the slightest reservation, I spoke my vow, too. "Yes, I accept Lucius as my husband, now and always, for as long as I shall exist."

Lucius smiled – as if he'd ever thought I'd *really* turn him down. Then we released our hands and both turned back toward Alexandru, who nodded first to Raniero, then to Mindy, signaling that they should reach for the small, silver cups filled with our blood.

CHAPTER 21

Although I tried hard to be alert to every detail of the rest of the ceremony – all of the things that happened after Lucius and I officially accepted each other – I only succeeded in capturing little moments here and there.

The instant when Mindy passed my cup to me, offering me my blood to share with Lucius, and the way he closed his eyes before he drank.

And when it was all over, I would recall finally noticing Raniero, and realizing that Lucius had somehow managed to get his best man cleaned up, so he looked suitably regal for a wedding. Mindy seemed to have noticed the change, too. I saw, once or twice, a familiar gleam in her eyes, like her "date" wasn't so bad, after all.

There were vivid images, too, of Alexandru opening the genealogy that Lucius had shown me months ago. The older vampire had slid the book across the stone table so I could sign my name next to my new husband's. Right before putting the pen to the yellowed paper, I'd turned to see my mom looking bravely happy, my dad crying, Dorin's eyes lit up with the history of the act, and Claudiu refusing to look at all, like he couldn't bear to see a Dragomir joining the Vladescu ranks.

All of those things went by so quickly, up until the moment Lucius slipped a wedding band onto my finger, and he held out his left hand to me.

Then, when our rings were in place, Alexandru Vladescu finally spoke the words I swore I couldn't wait one more second to hear. "Lucius, you may kiss your wife."

EPILOGUE

"Do you think we left the reception too early?" I asked Lucius, although I didn't really care if we'd been a little rude. I'd loved our party, which had taken place in a clearing high in the Carpathians – a place that I sometimes saw in dreams – but I'd been more than ready to go. "We didn't insult anyone, did we?"

Lucius looked down at me, but I could hardly see his face. We were walking through the dark forest, heading back to the estate, where we'd spend our honeymoon. "I think decorum was lost entirely, by everyone, somewhere around midnight," he said. "I believe it started with your father's dancing."

"That was some sort of tribal good luck thing he learned... somewhere," I defended Dad, even though I couldn't help laughing at the memory of the strange moves he'd attempted. And the spectacle had gotten worse when he'd drawn in my Uncle Dorin, who'd apparently had more than one glass of wine that evening.

Yes, that had probably marked the beginning of the end of the "stately" part of the reception.

"And then my best man and your maid of honor seemed to disappear without even a good-bye," Lucius noted.

I stopped laughing. That actually kind of worried me.

Had they really gone off together?

Before I could ask Lucius, for at least the tenth time, if we should go look for them – to which he would inevitably reply that I underestimated Mindy's and Raniero's good sense, in spite of the latter's bad taste in shorts – he added to my concerns.

"And last but not least, there was Claudiu's atrocious behavior toward you, throughout the evening. Behavior for which he will answer."

"Lucius, no." I didn't want to think about Claudiu right then, even if he had pretty much snubbed me at my own wedding. "Let's just let it go, okay?"

Lucius didn't say anything – didn't make a promise – and all at once it didn't matter so much. At least not right then, because we had stepped out of the woods and were crossing the last few yards to the castle.

When we reached the massive door, one of the guards, who had probably never been too far from us, materialized to open it, and Lucius bent down and swept me up off my feet, cradling me against his chest.

The gesture was clichéd enough to make us both laugh, but I'd secretly hoped that my new husband would carry me across the threshold.

We stopped talking, then, as Lucius carried me through the hallways, and I held tightly to him until we reached the door to the bedroom we'd share. Only this time there was no guard in sight. We were **really** alone.

He bent slightly to reach for the knob, twisted it and opened the door. Carrying me into the room, he set me gently down on to my feet, drew me to himself and said softly, "Welcome home, Antanasia."

Then Lucius reached back with one arm, still holding me with his other, and just as his lips touched mine, he closed the door behind us, shutting the world out.

ABOUT THE AUTHOR

Beth Fantaskey is the author of *Jessica's Guide to Dating on the Dark Side*, *Jessica Rules the Dark Side*, *Jekel Loves Hyde*, *Buzz Kill*, and *Isabel Feeney, Star Reporter*. Visit **bethfantaskeyauthor.com** for more information about her books, as well as study guides, short stories about your favorite characters and news about future interactive events.